Hello, Family Members,

Learning to read is one of the most important accomplishments of early childhood. **Hello Reader!** books are designed to help children become skilled readers who like to read. Beginning readers learn to read by remembering frequently used words like "the," "is," and "and"; by using phonics skills to decode new words; and by interpreting picture and text clues. These books provide both the stories children enjoy and the structure they need to read fluently and independently. Here are suggestions for helping your child *before*, *during*, and *after* reading:

Before

- Look at the cover and pictures and have your child predict what the story is about.
- Read the story to your child.
- Encourage your child to chime in with familiar words and phrases.
- Echo read with your child by reading a line first and having your child read it after you do.

During

- Have your child think about a word he or she does not recognize right away. Provide hints such as "Let's see if we know the sounds" and "Have we read other words like this one?"
- Encourage your child to use phonics skills to sound out new words.
- Provide the word for your child when more assistance is needed so that he or she does not struggle and the experience of reading with you is a positive one.
- Encourage your child to have fun by reading with a lot of expression . . . like an actor!

After

- Have your child keep lists of interesting and favorite words.
- Encourage your child to read the books over and over again. Have him or her read to brothers, sisters, grandparents, and even teddy bears. Repeated readings develop confidence in young readers.
- Talk about the stories. Ask and answer questions. Share ideas about the funniest and most interesting characters and events in the stories.

I do hope that you and your child enjoy this book.

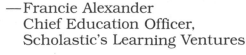

—Francie Alexander
   Chief Education Officer,
   Scholastic's Learning Ventures

To Justin Thomas
— M. P.

To my mom and dad
— C. G.

Go to scholastic.com for web site information on
Scholastic authors and illustrators.

ISBN 0-439-32097-6

Library of Congress Cataloging-in-Publication Data

Packard, Mary.
    Spring is here! / by Mary Packard; illustrated by Claudine Gévry.
    p. cm. – (Hello reader! Level 1)
    Summary: A girl enjoys the sights, sounds, and activities of springtime.
    ISBN 0-439-32097-6 (pbk.)
    [1. Spring—Fiction. 2. Stories in rhyme.]
    I. Gévry, Claudine, ill. II. Title. III. Series.
    PZ8.3.P125 Sp 2002
  [E] — dc21   2001042669

10   04 05 06
                        Printed in the U.S.A.
                        First printing, April 2002

SPRING IS HERE!

by Mary Packard
Illustrated by Claudine Gévry

Hello Reader! — Level 1

SCHOLASTIC INC. Cartwheel ·B·O·O·K·S·®

New York   Toronto   London   Auckland   Sydney
Mexico City   New Delhi   Hong Kong   Buenos Aires

Good-bye, winter.
Good-bye, snow.
Spring is on the way.

Hello, flowers!
Hello, sun!
Robin is here to stay.

Newborn chicks are in their nests
learning how to sing.

Ice cream trucks with ringing bells
are also signs of spring.

I love the sound my bat makes
when it hits the ball.

Of the many sounds of spring,
that one's best of all!

Swans and ducklings in the pond
follow one by one.

Tiny plants will grow so tall
in the bright, warm sun.

A soft, cool breeze lifts my kite
and messes up my hair.

Good-bye, coats.
Good-bye, hats.
Hello, warm spring air!

My mom packs a picnic lunch.
We eat it at the park.

It's fun to stay up with the sun
and play outside till dark.

Brand-new leaves in shades of green
pop out on every tree.

Then out burst soft, pink petals
to keep them company.

Flowers shoot up from the ground . . .

spreading color all around.

Raindrops make a splashy sound,
and everything looks new.

I love spring.
Do you?